DOCTOR·WHO

THE DARKSMITH LEGACY

D0191861

BBC CHILDREN'S BOOKS
Published by the Penguin Group
Penguin Books Ltd, 80 Strand, London, WC2R 0RL, England
Penguin Group (USA) Inc., 375 Hudson Street, New York 10014, USA
Penguin Books (Australia) Ltd, 250 Camberwell Road, Camberwell, Victoria 3124, Australia
(A division of Pearson Australia Group Pty Ltd)
Canada, India, New Zealand, South Africa
Published by BBC Children's Books, 2009
Text and design © Children's Character Books, 2009
This edition produced for The Book People Ltd,
Hall Wood Avenue, Haydock, St Helens, WA11 9UL
Written by Justin Richards
Cover illustration by Peter McKinstry
1
ISBN: 9781405906623
Printed in Great Britain by Clays Ltd, St Ives plc

DOCTOR·WHO

THE DARKSMITH LEGACY

THE DEPTHS OF DESPAIR

BY JUSTIN RICHARDS

Book
4

The Darksmith adventure continues online. Log on to
the website, enter the special codes from your book
and enjoy games and exclusive content about
The Darksmith Legacy.

www.thedarksmithlegacy.com

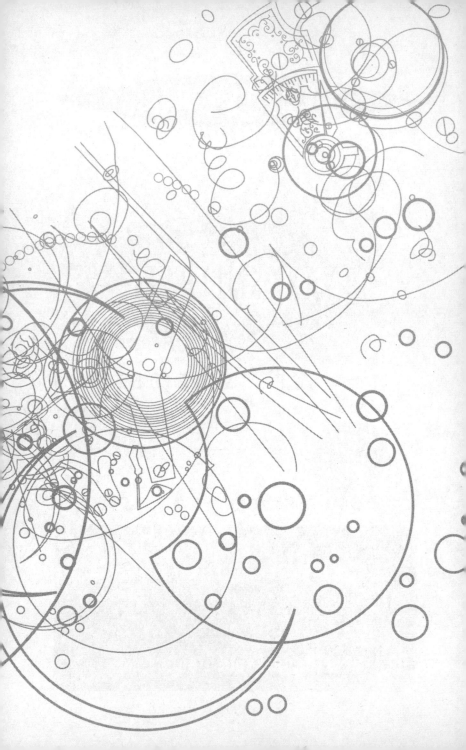

Contents

The Story So Far...

The Doctor has taken the powerful Eternity Crystal from the terrible Darksmith Collective on the planet Karagula. The Crystal can create life, and the Doctor knows it mustn't be allowed to fall into the wrong hands.

Varlos, the Darksmith who created the Crystal, realized this too. He stole the Crystal and fled from Karagula. The Darksmiths need the Crystal to fulfil their contract to create a device for a mysterious client. They also need Varlos as he is the only one who really understands how to make the device. The Doctor wants to find Varlos so he can discover how to destroy the powerful Crystal.

The Doctor knows that Varlos went to the planet Flydon Maxima – also known as Despair. But he doesn't know that the Darksmiths are tracking the TARDIS...

Straight into Trouble

A Darksmith wearing a cloak of emerald green, stepped forward – Brother Krazon, Minister for Justice.

'In the eyes of intergalactic law, the Doctor's removal of the Crystal, in the full knowledge of its rightful ownership by our Collective, constitutes common theft. And under Clause 374 of the Shadow Proclamation, "theft of an artefact of great cultural value legitimises the use of lethal force to ensure the artefact's recovery".'

High Minister Drakon's thin, colourless lips spread in a cruel sneer. 'Are you saying…'

'Yes, High Minister. We can lawfully set our Dreadbringers in pursuit of the Doctor.'

Drakon's eyes flared with malevolent passion. 'Do it, Krazon! I want the Dreadnought *Adamantine* space-worthy within the hour, carrying a full battalion of your finest soldiers.'

Brother Krazon nodded smartly, and hurried away.

Drakon looked back at the glowing blip on the scanner screen, slowly moving away from its centre, and gave another dry cackle. 'That's right, Doctor – run! Run as fast as you can. For, by stone and sun-fire, you have incurred the wrath of the Darksmiths of Karagula – and now your very nightmares are coming after you!'

The rasping, scraping sound of the TARDIS engines mixed with the constant howl of the cold wind. Misty air swirled above the thick ice. A few flakes of snow spun and twisted across the frozen landscape. The weak yellow sun made little impact on the vast cold wastes of the planet's northern pole.

The ice creaked. A crack appeared – sudden, like a gunshot. It spread quickly across the ice, as if a heavy weight had been dropped abruptly on to the surface. And the heavy weight of the TARDIS faded into existence. The ice cracked again, and the TARDIS leaned slightly. But the ice held.

The Doctor opened the door and stepped out of the TARDIS, standing at a slight angle like the TARDIS itself.

'Odd,' he murmured to himself. 'Everything's a

bit skew-whiff.' He straightened up. 'Oh yes. That's better.' Then he turned back to close the TARDIS door. 'Well, better for me anyway. You'll just have to live with it. Should be OK. Looks safe enough. I think.'

The Doctor jumped up and down on the ice. He started lightly, carefully at first – little more than bouncing on his feet. Then he risked a bit of a hop. Then a proper jump.

'Rock solid,' he decided. Just to be sure he hop-scotched across a section of the frozen ground.

'That's the problem with global warming,' he decided. 'Too much ice. It's weird that for an ice age to get started, the temperature has to rise. Just enough to get the glaciers moving. Still, on this planet they'll drown before they freeze.' He drew in a deep breath of cold air and blew out a mist of warmer air. 'Maybe not much of a comfort. And not a problem I have right now. But it's true, you know,' he announced to the empty wastes. 'I know, I read it somewhere.'

Then he stuffed his hands into his trouser pockets, and set off across the ice.

After a few minutes, the Doctor stopped walking.

TARDIS
Data Bank

The Oceans of Flydon Maxima

Flydon Maxima — also known as: 'Despair'

Part of the Flydon Agglomeration, the planet acquired its nickname from the attitude of the inhabitants when they discovered their planet was suffering from global warming created by pollution and carbon emissions. It was already past the point of no return before the population started to address the problem.

As the temperature rose, the polar caps started to melt and to move. The ice spread across the seas. As it thinned and melted, so the sea level rose.

Before the catastrophe, Flydon Maxima's surface was 88% water. To compare — planet Earth's surface is roughly 71% water.

As on Earth, the great oceans are composed of salt water and the currents greatly affected the planet's climate. Also as on Earth, the oceans are tidal. The tides are the rising and falling of the ocean's surface caused by the gravitational pull of the planet's sun and its single moon.

The rise of the seas meant that the entire planet was soon covered with water. The population was forced to adapt. Some lived in great floating cities, struggling to survive on fish and seaweed, collecting rainwater to drink. Others were able to evacuate to the smaller nearby planet of Flydon Minima.

He buttoned up his coat and did a little jogging on the spot. Then he blew into his hands and blew out another long misty breath. Finally, he took his sonic screwdriver from his inside pocket.

'Oh,' the Doctor said as he checked the readings he was getting. 'Oh,' he said again when he realized they were right. 'So I need to be heading, er, straight… down.' He looked at his feet. He stamped them a bit. 'TARDIS,' he decided. 'Not going to be able to walk there. Wherever *there* is.'

There was an energy source and heat. It was where the people were, he hoped. The Doctor had set the TARDIS to land about half a mile away from the exact co-ordinates he had managed to derive from a lengthy examination of Varlos' data, so as not to draw unwanted attention. He hadn't expected that to mean he'd arrive half a mile *above* where he wanted to be. He turned and headed back towards the TARDIS, kicking at tufts of snow and sending up swirling clouds.

It was a bright, clear day and the Doctor had a good view of the TARDIS as he approached it. The blue was dark against the brilliant white of the ice around it. The TARDIS was still leaning slightly to one side. As the Doctor watched, it slipped slightly more.

'Whoops!' the Doctor broke into a run. 'No you don't!' he shouted as the TARDIS slipped further sideways. What was making that happen, he wondered. It wasn't *that* heavy – the ice must be metres thick beneath it.

Then, in a sudden explosion of ice and water, the Doctor had his answer.

The whole surface of the ice between the Doctor and the TARDIS erupted. Water sprayed up like a geyser. And in the middle of it a writhing mass of tentacles clawed up through the hole they had made and spread rapidly across the ice – probing, feeling, searching.

One of the tentacles slapped down near the Doctor. The ice cracked beneath its massive weight. The tentacle was as thick as the Doctor's body. One side of it was mottled brown, the other was studded with suckers that shimmered and throbbed as they convulsed, latching on to the ice as the enormous creature heaved itself up and out of the depths.

The Doctor stood and stared. 'Oh what are *you*?' he wondered out loud. He could see a large, bulbous body at the heart of the mass of tentacles now. 'Giant octopus?' he wondered. 'No, too many tentacles.

Far too many. Multi-pus maybe. Dodecapus would have twelve limbs, I think you're way beyond that. Tell you what,' he went on, jumping back to avoid the tentacle that was thrashing around close by, 'I'll just wait here till you're done with whatever you're doing. Then I'll get back to my TARDIS and be out of your way. How's that?'

As if in answer, the tentacle withdrew. The Doctor grinned happily. But his grin rapidly became a frown as he saw that the massive creature was now reaching out for the TARDIS. A tentacle stroked it down the front, feeling the light, the windows, the door handles. Another was slowly curling round the back of the TARDIS as if the monstrous creature was about to hug it tight.

Then he realized the situation was even worse than that. Slowly but surely, the creature was withdrawing, sinking back down through the ice into the water far below. And it was dragging the TARDIS with it.

Beneath the Ice

The Doctor had just moments to act. Otherwise he'd lose the TARDIS, perhaps forever.

The only way to get to the door was to go *over* the monster. The Doctor would have to take a run at it, and use the thrashing tentacles as stepping stones to get to the door before the TARDIS was dragged down through the ice. But which was the quickest path?

The first step was the worst. The Doctor sprinted across the cracking ice and jumped on to the tentacle. It compressed and squelched under his foot, and he almost stumbled. But he managed to keep going. It wasn't so very different from his earlier game of hopscotch, he thought. Except the creature had felt his feet on its flesh, and the tentacle he was running along was moving.

Activity

Which tentacle should the Doctor follow to get to the TARDIS as quickly as he can before it is dragged under the ice?

A

B

C

D

E

F

G

Enter your answer

_____

He launched himself forwards, and managed to reach the edge of the TARDIS. Perched on the door sill, he fumbled for the key. The door swung open and the Doctor tumbled inside.

'Third tentacle from the left,' he said breathlessly as he closed the door on the mass of tentacles trying to get in. He stood with his back leaning on the door for a moment. 'I should have known. It's *always* the third tentacle from the left.'

The TARDIS lurched, and the Doctor was thrown sideways. It was time to be going.

The floor was shaking under his feet as he staggered to the TARDIS console. He pushed the sonic screwdriver into a recess in the console. This time he'd go straight to Varlos' co-ordinates, and worry about being conspicuous later.

The central column rose and fell, and the Doctor let out a sigh of relief and anticipation.

In the icy polar wastes of the planet known as Despair, an enormous creature found that its tentacles were suddenly empty. The strange blue object it had found on the ice was inexplicably gone. One moment it was there, the next it was not.

Confused, the creature slipped back into the

ocean depths. As soon as it was gone, the surface water began to freeze again. Soon the hole it had made would be gone too...

The TARDIS' next landing place was very different from the icy wastes. It materialised in a gloomy maintenance area. Pipes ran round the walls – dripping and corroded. The floor was a rusty metal mesh that the water seeped through. The walls were sweating with condensation. Or just possibly, the Doctor thought, leaking in water from the ocean outside. It was, after all, half a mile under water.

Whistling a hornpipe, the Doctor locked the TARDIS and set off in search of anyone or anything interesting. He didn't have to go far.

The door from the maintenance area was heavy, round and watertight, like an airlock or the doors of a submarine. The Doctor swung the locking wheel and stepped through into a passageway. He closed and sealed the door behind him. Maybe the place did leak after all – but whether it did or not it was good practice to keep the doors closed and sealed.

He had a choice of directions. The Doctor licked his finger and held it up. Then he nodded, as if that told him something useful – which it didn't – and set off to the left. He was still whistling as he reached another very similar locked door at the end of the passage.

But before the Doctor could open the door, the locking wheel began to turn of its own accord. Or rather, the Doctor realized, because someone was trying to open it from the other side. He positioned himself so it wouldn't bump into him when it opened and leaned nonchalantly against the wall of the passageway as the door swung open.

The figure that stepped through was a little old man in grimy overalls. He was wearing a peaked cap, and carrying a battered metal toolbox. He stared at the Doctor through pale, surprised eyes and wiped a wrinkled hand over his badly-shaven face.

'Who the blooming Nora are you?' the man demanded in a cracked voice.

'Nope,' the Doctor said, pushing himself away from the wall. 'Not Nora. Doctor. Doctor Smith. Here from the um – you know.' He flashed his psychic paper at the man and let that do the talking for him. It would show the man something he was expecting to see, something that would explain why the Doctor was here.

'Not another ruddy inspection,' the man complained.

'Oh yes,' the Doctor told him happily. 'Another ruddy inspection. Now, who the blooming Nora are you and where do we ruddy get started?'

The man was called Hank and he was responsible for the maintenance of the scientific base the Doctor was now in.

Hank led the Doctor to the main crew lounge where he said everyone else would be as it was a break.

'Break for everyone else, anyhow,' he said gloomily. 'Doesn't look like I get a break. Always something that needs sorting or mending or fixing or putting back together.'

'But you do it so well,' the Doctor told him. 'I was looking back through the last set of inspection results and they gave you a commendation.'

'They what?'

'Richly deserved,' the Doctor went on quickly. 'It's obvious only because of you that this place keeps going at all.'

'That's true enough,' Hank admitted. 'But try telling Captain Strova.'

They had arrived at another of the sealed metal

doors, and Hank put down his tool box to work the locking wheel.

'Difficult to work with, is he?' the Doctor asked as the door swung open.

On the other side of the door was a tall woman wearing a green military uniform. Her hair was cut short and her features were thin and pinched as she stared in surprise at the Doctor. A nametag sewn over her breast pocket said: STROVA.

'*She*,' the Doctor corrected himself. 'Difficult to work with is she?' His voice tailed off as he realized what he was saying. 'Your auntie,' he added quickly. 'We were just talking about Hank's Auntie Nora. Lovely woman. Have you met her? Well, I say lovely, she can be a bit difficult at times, but – hey – can't we all? I'm the Doctor. Here to do a snap inspection. So, you'd be Captain Strova, would you?'

The military woman's eyes narrowed slightly. 'I'm Strova,' she said. 'And I warn you, I can be difficult to work with.'

The Doctor's eyes widened. 'Really? You don't look the type.'

As he was speaking, the woman's mouth twitched, and then she smiled. 'Just kidding.

Another inspection? Hank didn't tell me there was someone on their way down in a capsule. But come in and meet the crew. We're on a break.'

She led the Doctor into the room. Hank did not follow. 'I'm off to check on Airlock 3,' he said glumly. 'Like anyone's interested.'

The room was quite large, and furnished with several battered armchairs and an old sofa. It looked more like a school staff room than an underwater base. There was a little kitchen area with a kettle and toaster above what looked like a fridge. Off to the side was a wall of metal lockers.

A dining table stood in an alcove. On it the Doctor could see what looked like a lump of coral – a pale, gnarled and twisted formation with spikes and nodules. There were other bits of the same material on various surfaces round the room, presumably as decoration.

'He never stops, poor Hank,' Captain Strova said. 'I don't think he likes to take a break. But to be fair, if it wasn't for him this place wouldn't work at all. He keeps it going pretty much single-handedly. But don't tell him that,' she added in a pretend whisper. The Doctor laughed. 'I think he enjoys being gloomy and having something to complain about.'

'You're not wrong there,' said another voice. A man was getting up from one of the armchairs. There was another man in the room, getting something out of the fridge. Both were wearing similar uniforms to Strova.

'Private Lenk,' the man who had spoken introduced himself. 'And that's Private Rodoff.'

The man at the fridge waved. 'Hi.'

The Doctor almost missed the other person in the room. A young girl. She was sitting at the dining table, examining a collection of papers that was spread across it. The girl looked up at the Doctor, tilting her head slightly to one side as she examined him.

The girl seemed to be about eleven years old. She had a very round, pale and delicate face with big, dark eyes. Her coal black hair was cut in a perfect bob.

'And this, of course, is Gisella,' Captain Strova said.

'Of course,' the Doctor said. He walked over to the girl, hoping he didn't intimidate her. 'Hi, I'm the Doctor. So what are you doing here?' he asked in is best and most friendly 'talking to children' voice.

He glanced at the papers on the table, expecting them to be drawings or perhaps the first few pages of a soon-to-be-abandoned story.

But the papers were covered with numbers and equations. There were tables of water pressures, temperature readings, sensor information…

'I never bothered with a doctorate,' the girl said in a slightly disapproving tone. 'I never seemed to have the time. If you're really here to do an inspection, then you know who I am and what I'm doing here. I'm Gisella, and I'm in charge of this base.'

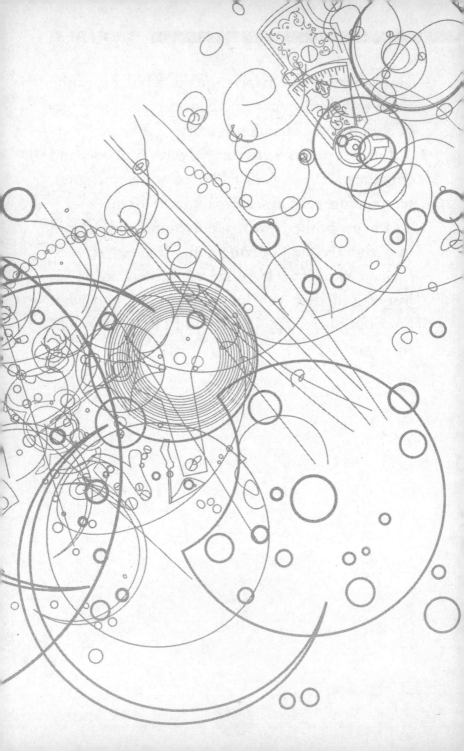

Guided Tour

The Doctor did his best to hide his surprise. 'Gisella – of course. I know all about you. Well,' he admitted, 'not all about you. But enough. Just the right amount, in fact. And I know you're in charge.'

He turned to catch Captain Strova's eye. 'She's in charge?' he mouthed, making sure that Gisella couldn't see him.

Captain Strova smiled. 'You'll also know, Doctor,' she said, 'that Gisella is older than she looks. She has a rare condition – a unique condition – known as *Adulescentia Perpetuus*.'

'Perpetual youth,' the Doctor translated. 'She never gets old.'

'Hey,' Private Lenk called across, 'I bet you wish you suffered from that!'

The Doctor returned his grin, but there was a sadness deep behind his eyes. 'Oh, I'm sure there are disadvantages.' He turned back to Gisella. 'Like pompous doctors treating you as if you really are a child.'

Gisella returned his stare. 'You get used to it,' she said. 'I bet people treat you like an idiot.'

'Yeah they do, actually,' the Doctor admitted. 'How did you guess that?'

'But you're not an idiot at all,' the little girl who wasn't a little girl went on. 'Though sometimes you want people to think you are. Sometimes you play to your image.'

The Doctor nodded, any trace of idiocy completely gone. 'Sometimes,' he said seriously. 'So – you want an ice cream and a game of tiddlywinks, or what?'

The sudden return of his grin helped to make the moment funny, and they all laughed – including the Doctor and Gisella.

'It's difficult for us too,' Private Rodoff said. 'Being ordered about by someone who looks like a child.'

The Doctor nodded. 'Or inspected by someone who acts like an idiot?'

'I didn't say that,' Rodoff said.

'You didn't have to,' Captain Strova told him.

The Doctor flopped down in one of the armchairs, stretching his long legs out in front of him. 'Well, how about we keep going with the idiot thing?' he suggested. 'Just pretend I know nothing at all about what's going on here. Give me the whole story, right from the start.' He suddenly drew in his legs and sat upright. 'Oh, and if there's any chance of a cup of tea, that'd be great. I'm parched.'

Rodoff made the Doctor a mug of tea and set it down on a low table beside the armchair. Beside the mug was one of the strange-shaped pieces of coral. The Doctor picked it up and examined it while he listened to Captain Strova and Gisella explain about the underwater base, and waited for his tea to cool.

'This base was set up a hundred and fifty years ago,' Strova explained. 'Back when Flydon Maxima was still inhabited. Global warming had started, and they realized they were in big trouble.'

'Only they didn't realize how big,' Private Lenk put in. 'A hundred years later, and we'd all had to evacuate to Flydon Minima.'

'So what's it for, why's it still here?' the Doctor

wondered. 'Why are you lot here?'

'To learn,' Gisella told him. 'The water is still rising, the effects of the atmospheric pollution and the carbon emissions are still being felt. It's our job to monitor it and track what's happening.'

'Out of scientific curiosity?' the Doctor asked.

'Partly. And so we can learn more about what we've done to this planet. So we can make sure we don't do it again.'

'We are also surveying and cataloguing the marine life,' Strova said. 'We monitor what's going on in the water, and we are constantly measuring the thickness of the ice crust above us, measuring the pressure it exerts on the water, the exact temperature, everything.'

The Doctor sipped his tea. It was a bit weak and milky, but it was warm. 'So what's this stuff?' he asked, holding up the lump of coral.

'We think it's volcanic sediment,' Gisella said. 'Extruded rock. Molten lava bubbles up from a fissure, then when it hits the water, it cools rapidly and solidifies into these strange shapes.'

'I found a whole cave full of the stuff on the seabed,' Rodoff said. 'The last time I was out checking the probes.'

34

'The seabed shifts,' Strova said. 'Earthquakes, volcanic activity. We're forever having to go out and replace or repair probes, or plant new ones in new survey sites.'

'Keeps you busy, I imagine,' the Doctor said. 'This tea's very good, thank you.' He finished it and put the mug down again next to the volcanic rock that looked like coral. 'It's certainly distinctive. Talking of which, and about monitoring sea life…'

'Yes?' Gisella said.

'I met an interesting example of sea life when I arrived on the ice.' He pointed upwards. 'Big fellow, he was. Lots of tentacles. Quite friendly. Well, I say friendly – he tried to give me a hug. Love-you-to-death sort of friendly.'

'That'd be a Blaska,' Lenk said. 'Sort of cross between an octopus and a jellyfish.'

'First catalogued by Theodore Blaska,' Gisella explained.

'They can get a bit angry if you get in their way,' Captain Strova said.

'I noticed,' the Doctor told her.

'They've got worse recently,' Lenk went on. 'They used to leave us alone, and keep well away. But now there are several outside the base all the time. Like they're just waiting for us to come out so they can get us.'

'I'm not going out there again unless I have to,' Rodoff said. 'Hank reckons they're going to attack the base.'

'We've been here a hundred and fifty years,' Gisella said, 'and there's no record of them ever attacking the base.'

'Well, I tell you one of them nearly got me in that cave,' Rodoff said. He shivered at the memory. 'It was completely mad. I was lucky to get out at all.'

'If you've finished your tea, Doctor,' Strova said, 'do you want to start your inspection?'

The Doctor jumped to his feet. 'Love to,' he said. 'Delighted. Can't wait. Allons-y!'

The equipment that monitored the water around the base and the ice shelf high above it was automatic. Hank was responsible for keeping it running, while Gisella took readings and analysed them.

The Doctor was surprised and impressed at how much of the analysis and calculation she did in her head, but she also wrote computer programs that were run on massive server systems that were kept in a huge machine room deep under the base.

Strova and Gisella took him down to the machine room. It was a vast, open area. Huge columns held up the base above, but that still left a huge space – a huge space filled with computers and data storage and monitoring equipment. The Doctor examined everything, and it didn't take him long to be sure that much of the equipment was built using technology developed by the Darksmiths.

'So, where did it all come from?' the Doctor asked. 'When the base was set up a hundred and fifty years ago, where did they get all this equipment?'

'Gisella's been here longer than anyone,' Strova said. 'Do you know?' she asked Gisella. 'There must be some record.'

'I just wondered,' the Doctor said.

Gisella was looking intently at the Doctor through her big, dark eyes. He sensed she could tell there was more to his question than there seemed. 'It was donated by someone,' she said.

'Very generous. Did this someone have a name?'

'He donated some of the more advanced equipment,' Gisella said. 'He helped set up the base and set down some rules about the staffing. I think his name was Varlos.'

The Doctor nodded. He adjusted a setting on

one of the computer consoles, tapped the readout dial on another. 'And I'm guessing he wasn't local.'

Gisella's expression didn't alter. 'I wouldn't know,' she said.

'Of course not,' the Doctor said, with just enough sarcasm that the girl would know he could tell she was lying.

But before she could answer, a loud tone echoed round the room. It was followed by Rodoff's voice, loud and distorted through intercom speakers close to the ceiling.

'Captain Strova, Gisella – this is Rodoff. I'm in the Observation Gallery with Hank. I think you'd better get up here. We've got a problem.'

Rodoff's voice cut off, and was replaced by Hank's: 'Give me that. I'll say we've got a problem. I told you those things were trouble. There are three Blaska outside, and it looks like they're about to attack.'

'Look out!' Rodoff's voice shouted through the speakers.

There was a sudden crash of sound, then the speakers cut out. There was silence, broken only by the hum of the machinery and the Doctor's running footsteps.

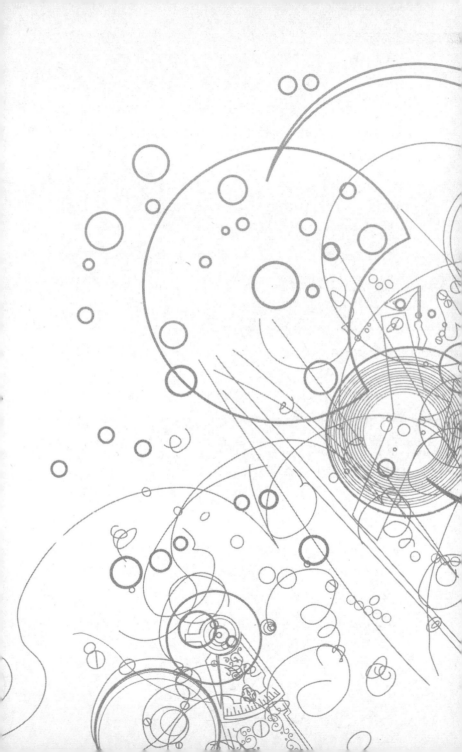

Flood Warning

'**W**hich way?' the Doctor shouted when he got to the top of the steps out of the Machine Room. It was frustrating, but he had to wait for Captain Strova to catch up with him. Little Gisella was struggling to keep up.

Together, they ran through the base. There were heavy watertight doors at regular intervals, and Strova insisted they close and seal each door behind them as they went. The Doctor knew the doors could be opened and closed automatically from the Machine Room. But unless one of them was going to stay behind and operate the doors, that didn't really help.

After what seemed like an age, they arrived at the Observation Gallery. It was situated right at the top of the spherical underwater base. The curved walls and domed ceiling were made of glass – or something incredibly strong that was just as clear. Finito-glass, probably, the Doctor thought as he hurried into the enormous room.

'What's going on?' Strova demanded. 'Are you OK?'

Hank and Rodoff were standing in the middle of the room. By way of answer, Rodoff pointed upwards. High above them, at the top of the dome, there was a crack. It wasn't very big, little more than a star-shaped blemish on the glass. But as they all watched, it grew. With a sound like cracking ice, the star shape expanded outwards. A spider's web shot out, spreading across the glass.

'How did that happen?' Gisella asked.

'I think we're about to find out,' the Doctor said.

He could see a shape moving in the distance behind the glass. A mass of writhing tentacles round a bulbous body. It was growing rapidly larger as it approached – rushing towards the glass. It was aiming for the centre of the web of cracks, hurling itself at the base. In the distance behind it, the Doctor could see another of the Blaska creatures. And behind that, a third.

'Oh, that's not good,' the Doctor murmured.

'Not good at all.'

The first Blaska hit the glass with a sound like thunder. The creature's tentacles curled round the dome, suckers flat against the glass like hundreds of mouths. The tendrils inside each sucker were like tiny teeth. The main body of the Blaska hammered into the glass at exactly the point where the cracks started.

Immediately the cracks spread. Something dropped on to the Doctor's face. He wiped at it with his hand. Water.

The Blaska was sliding off the glass dome, gathering itself and swimming away – ready for another go. The second Blaska was already hurtling rapidly at the same point high above.

A trickle of water was drip-drip-dripping at the Doctor's feet. When the next Blaska hit…

'Out!' the Doctor yelled. 'Everyone – out! The roof's going to go.'

The Doctor gathered Gisella as he ran, scooping her off her feet. She was heavier than she looked, and he almost fell as he took her weight. As she resisted him, for just a second before realizing he was helping her, she was stronger than she looked. Much, much stronger.

But there was no time to think about that. The Doctor was through the door, Captain Strova close behind him. Rodoff and Hank raced through after them. The Doctor put Gisella down and slammed the heavy door shut. As it closed, he caught the briefest glimpse of the second Blaska impacting on the domed roof. There was split-second view of the entire glass dome shattering and raining down – a lethal mixture of broken glass and tonnes of water.

Then the door slammed shut. The Doctor was spinning the locking wheel. The whole structure shuddered under the weight of the mass of water crashing against the door.

'That was close,' Rodoff said.

'It's not over yet,' Hank told him gloomily.

As if in answer, the door shuddered again. A drip of water escaped from the sealed edge and splashed to the floor.

'If they can break through three metres of finito-glass,' Gisella said, 'they can easily get through that door.'

'There must be something that can hold them,' the Doctor said. 'Don't tell me these watertight doors are the only protection the base has against catastrophic failure?'

'We didn't expect the Blaska to attack,' Rodoff pointed out. 'They never have before. The first time any of them was really aggressive was when it cornered me in the cave last week.'

'Doesn't help,' the Doctor told him. He had to shout above the sound of hammering on the other side of the door. 'Right now we either need to escape from this base, or we need to take refuge in an area with rather better protection.'

'Level 3,' Gisella said. 'Green Area. If we can get there before they do.' She pointed at the door. Water was spraying round the edges now, and the middle was dented and buckled.

'Quickest way is down through the Machine Room and up the service stairs,' Hank said. 'There's a freight capsule that goes up to the surface from the Green Area, we can seal ourselves inside Level 3 and if we have to we can escape and launch a distress beacon into orbit.'

They were already running as Hank spoke. Captain Strova was talking urgently into a radio microphone attached to her lapel, telling Private Lenk what was happening and where they were headed.

'So why is this Green Area on Level 3 so secure?'

the Doctor wondered.

Before anyone could answer, there was a terrific crash from behind them, followed by the roar of the water rushing through the doorway.

The next door opened towards them, and Hank was holding it back as water surged down the corridor. A tentacle lashed out, almost catching Gisella as she dived through after Strova and Rodoff. The Doctor waved for Hank to go through, then followed.

He didn't need to pull the door shut – it was a struggle to keep it open while he ducked through. Then the door slammed behind him. There was no point it locking it. The Doctor ran after the others. But he knew that next time, it might be closer – the Blaska would have a better idea of how to break through now.

Through another two doors, the water close behind them each time, and then they were clattering down the steps to the Machine Room.

'What happens when this place floods?' the Doctor wondered.

'I'd rather not think about it,' Hank replied. 'But the Green Area has backup systems. If we can get there.'

'Let me buy us some time then,' the Doctor said, hurrying to the nearest computer terminal. 'Maybe more than that, if we're lucky.'

'What are you doing?' Strova demanded.

Gisella could see that the Doctor had opened a schematic plan of the base. 'He's opening some of the watertight doors,' she realized.

'Stop him – he'll flood the place,' Rodoff yelled, rushing at the Doctor.

But Strova caught him and held him back. 'No, leave him.'

'I'm only opening *some* of the doors,' the Doctor said as he worked frantically. 'Let's hope those Blaska creatures hunt or whatever they're doing by instinct. They'll follow the water, the path of least resistance. If I can get them to this point here, then they might break through Airlock 2 and just leave.' He pointed to one of the airlocks at the end of the trail of doors he was opening. Blue shading showed the path of the water as it flooded through.

'The problem is,' Gisella said, 'you need to clear a path to the airlock without flooding either this Machine Room, or the path we need to take from the access stairs to the Green Area.'

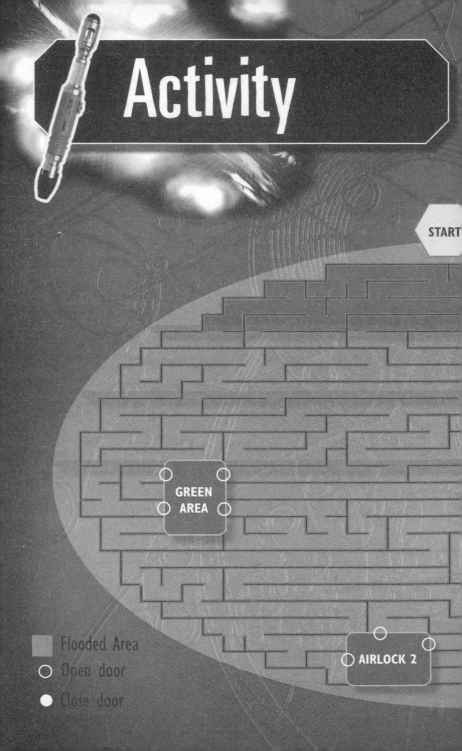

Activity

START

GREEN
AREA

Flooded Area
○ Open door
● Close door

AIRLOCK 2

Indentify the watertight doors you need to open to clear a path from the water to Airlock 2. Be careful not to let water flood into the Machine Room or the Green Area on level 3, or the route between them.

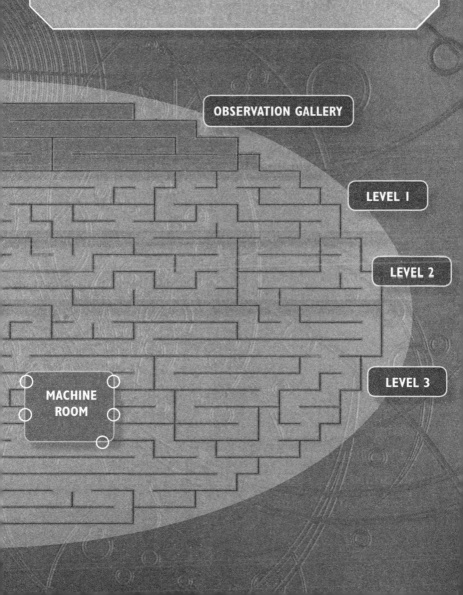

OBSERVATION GALLERY

LEVEL 1

LEVEL 2

LEVEL 3

MACHINE ROOM

'Will it work?' Hank asked. 'Will those things just follow the water?'

'Depends what they're really after and why they decided to attack the base,' the Doctor said. 'Right, that should do it.'

He watched with satisfaction as the last door opened automatically, and the plan of the base showed where the water was flowing – all the way from the Observation Gallery to Airlock 2, but without endangering the Machine Room or the Green Area, or the route they would need to take to get from one to the other.

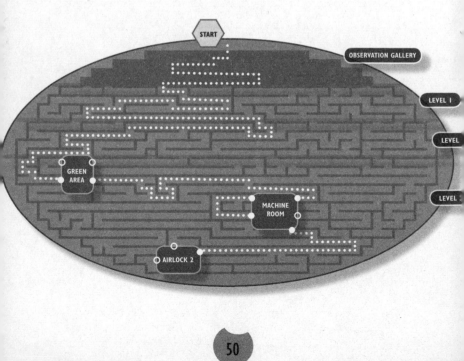

'Right, let's get going,' Strova said. 'Lenk should be powering up the secondary systems in the Green Area by now.'

'You never told me,' the Doctor said. 'What's in this Green Area place? Why is it so much more secure than anywhere else?'

'It's behind blast doors,' Rodoff said. 'The walls are three metres thick and lined with lead.'

'It's the nuclear reactor that powers the base,' Gisella told them. 'If those creatures get in there, then we won't need to worry about drowning. The whole place will explode.'

Ice Strike

Water was leaking in. The floors were damp, and the walls and ceilings were dripping.

'I hope those doors hold,' Gisella said. 'We can check when we get to the Green Area what the pressure readings are.'

'We'll know if the Blaska have followed the path the Doctor made and gone back into the ocean,' Captain Strova added.

'If they haven't we're in trouble,' Hank said.

'Always looking on the bright side,' the Doctor answered cheerily. 'Where's your sense of optimism?'

'It was sent home by my sense of realism,' Hank replied.

They reached Level 3 without incident, and Captain Strova led the way to the Green Area. The

Doctor could tell that they had arrived because the corridor they were in ended in massive lead-lined doors. They were much thicker and heavier than the standard watertight doors throughout the rest of the base. A security keypad was set into the wall beside the doors.

'What if the power fails, or we flood?' the Doctor asked as Gisella typed in a code.

'The doors automatically close and lock if the power goes off,' she said. 'There's a hydraulic pump you can work by hand to open them again. The same code opens the combination lock on it.'

The massive metals doors were swinging slowly open. Private Lenk was standing on the other side of them. He looked relieved that they had finally arrived.

'Everything's powered up,' Lenk said.

Gisella hurried past him into the control room beyond. 'Then let's see what's going on.'

The Green Area was dominated by a huge metal cylinder that stood in the middle. The Doctor knew it was the containment vessel for the nuclear reactor housed inside. There were control consoles and computer terminals all round the room. Most of them were blank and silent. But Gisella was already at one of the active terminals.

The Doctor hurried to join her. 'How are we doing?'

'Not good. Look – the Blaska are still inside the base.'

Gisella had a schematic plan of the base open on the screen – similar to the one the Doctor had worked on in the Machine Room. She pointed to where a door had been opened – a door that was not on the Doctor's path to Airlock 2.

'Why have they gone that way?' the Doctor wondered.

Are they looking for us?' Strova asked, looking over Gisella's shoulder at the screen.

As they watched, another door failed. The symbol blinked and went out.

'They're heading for the living quarters,' Gisella said.

'But they can't know that,' the Doctor pointed out. '*They* don't have a plan of the base. Oh, they might be able to sense its form, maybe using sonar or echo-sounding or something. They might work out the shape of the corridors and rooms. But they don't know what you use them for.'

'Can they sense *us*?' Rodoff asked nervously.

'If they can, then we're toast,' Hank said glumly.

'Don't be daft,' the Doctor retorted. 'How can we be toast? They'd need a toaster – a very big toaster. A toaster the size of...' He looked round, trying to decide how big a toaster it would actually have to be. As he did so, he caught sight of the huge containment vessel in front of them. 'Ah,' the Doctor said. 'I see. Yes, you're right. They come to get us, and this whole place is probably toast. Good point,' he added. 'Not terribly uplifting, but good. That'll be your realism taking charge again.'

'So what's the plan?' Lenk asked. 'We just wait here to get toasted or drowned? Is there anything we can do? That's what I want to know.'

The Doctor tapped his sonic screwdriver against his chin as he watched the readings on the screen. 'What *I* want to know is,' he said quietly, 'what's that?' He pointed with the sonic screwdriver at a readout.

Gisella frowned, working at the controls. 'That's the pressure of the water above us. It's changing. Like there's something pressing down on it.'

Captain Strova was working at one of the other consoles. 'I've got a collision alarm,' she called urgently. 'There's something heading straight for us!'

'Another Blaska?' the Doctor asked, running over to join her.

'No, wrong shape. It's not organic, not an animal. Heavy, solid…' She checked another reading. 'And going to hit the base in five seconds.'

'Hold on tight!' the Doctor shouted. He grabbed the control console in front of him and braced himself.

Everyone else was holding tight to the nearest fixed object – control consoles, safety rails, bulkheads.

Then it hit.

The whole room shook. The floor seemed to drop away for a second. The walls shuddered. The ceiling creaked ominously.

'There's more coming,' Strova shouted. 'Smaller. Like pieces of something.'

The Doctor was braced at the console, studying the readings. 'Hydrogen-oxygen mixture,' he read aloud. 'That can't be right. It's *water*.'

'That was never water,' Gisella told him.

'Oh yes it was. Frozen water. Ice!'

The room shook again, but less violently this time.

'Ice?' Hank said. 'But ice floats.'

'That's right,' the Doctor agreed. 'But a whole section of the ice shelf above us just sheared off. It fell into the water and its weight carried it down this deep.' He pointed to a readout. 'Look, its rising again now.'

'But what could make that happen?' Lenk wanted to know. 'Is it just the warming, or what?' The Doctor shook his head. 'Something hit the ice from above. Something heavy knocked into it and forced it down.'

They were all looking up at the ceiling of the room as the Doctor spoke.

'There's something up there,' he said.

The Doctor was keen to go on his own, but Gisella insisted. Strova wanted to come too, but Gisella ordered her to stay with the others.

'We can't survive up there in the cold for more than a few hours. And I want you down here, in case the Blaska find us.'

It was odd, the Doctor thought, to see a little girl giving orders to an experienced solder. But then, the Doctor reminded himself, there was more to Gisella than there seemed. A lot more. Something to discuss on the journey up to the surface.

It would have been easier and quicker to take the TARDIS. But it was on the other side of the base, and he didn't fancy trying to sneak past the angry Blaska that were still making their way towards the living quarters. There was a method in their progress – it was deliberate, planned. What were they doing? One problem at a time, he told himself. For now, whatever was happening on the surface was more important.

'Maybe it's a rescue ship,' Hank suggested in a rare moment of optimism.

'They'd have signalled,' Rodoff said.

'Maybe they did,' Lenk told him. 'We've been kind of busy with other things.'

Hank led the Doctor and Gisella round the cylindrical containment vessel until they arrived at what looked like sliding lift doors.

'Elevator?' the Doctor asked.

'Pressure capsule,' Hank said. He frowned. 'But you know that – you came down in one, surely.'

The Doctor grinned. 'Of course. Sealed box with double doors on the front. Absolutely that's how I got here.' He stepped inside. 'Coming, Gisella? Heading for the top floor, I assume.'

The controls were like buttons in an elevator. The top one was marked 'Surface' and the Doctor pressed it. The doors closed, and he felt the floor judder under his feet. A small screen showed the capsule as a yellow blob, moving slowly up from an image of the base towards a line that represented the surface.

'Going up,' the Doctor said happily. 'How long will it take?'

'A few minutes,' Gisella replied.

'Time for a chat, then. So – how long have you been here on the base?'

'Long enough.'

The Doctor nodded. 'That long? I ask, because – well, a couple of reasons really.'

'Such as?'

'Such as, I think you know more about Varlos than you're letting on.'

Gisella didn't reply for a moment. Then she said: 'That's only one reason.'

'Another would be that I've never heard of *Adulescentia Perpetuus*. I don't believe there's any such condition.'

Gisella's expression didn't change. 'Like Strova said, I'm unique. The only one of my kind.'

'Something else you and I have in common,' the Doctor said. 'So tell me about Varlos. I came here to find him. I need his help, and I think he needs mine.'

'And you think I can help you find him?'

'Can you?'

Gisella opened her mouth to reply. But at that moment, the capsule slowed and stopped. The doors slid slowly open.

The capsule had emerged from the ice and was standing on the surface rather like a small, square, metal hut. Snow was blowing across the icy landscape. But even through the snow, the Doctor and Gisella could see at once what had made the ice collapse and fall.

The Dreadbringers

Standing on the ice, braced and supported by enormous metal struts that stuck out like legs from its side, was what looked like a cathedral. It was made of stone so pale it looked like bone. The shape was almost lost against the snow and ice. A central tower rose high into the cold air. Windows of toughened glass, braced with metal were dark against the stonework.

'What is it?' Gisella asked.

'Trouble,' the Doctor said quietly.

At the front of the structure was a huge door. As the Doctor and Gisella watched it swing down, crashing on to the ice. Moments later, a line of figures emerged. They marched from the cathedral-like spaceship in a well-disciplined line. They were tall, broad-shouldered figures wearing dark cloaks

63

over their battle armour. The leading figure had the hood of his cloak pushed back, to reveal the black, angular helmet that covered his head. He held a long staff, and the breastplate of his armour was emblazoned with a crimson shield struck through with a dark flame.

'What are they?' Gisella said. 'What are they doing here?'

As she spoke, the leading figure turned slowly towards them, looking out across the icy landscape to where the Doctor and Gisella were standing just inside the capsule.

'They're Dreadbringers,' the Doctor said. 'And they're here for me.'

The leading Dreadbringer raised the staff he was holding, and pointed it at the Doctor and Gisella. Even at a distance, the Doctor could see the end of the staff glow a livid red.

He pushed Gisella to one side. A moment later the back of the capsule behind them exploded. The smoke cleared, leaving a black stain across the metal.

'Time we were going,' the Doctor said, stabbing at the control buttons with his index finger.

The doors closed agonisingly slowly. Another bolt

of energy hammered into them before they were fully shut, the sound echoing round the capsule. The last thing the Doctor saw before the doors came together was another line of Dreadbringers marching from their stone ship.

'We'll be safe in the base,' Gisella said. Then she saw the Doctor's expression. 'Won't we? I mean, they can't get down through the water.'

'They got down through the atmosphere,' the Doctor said. 'Not that I think they'll bring their whole great big stone spaceship down through the water.'

As he spoke he was working with the sonic screwdriver, aiming it at the small screen that showed the position of the capsule as it dropped slowly back towards the base. The image flickered and several more yellow blobs appeared. They were above the capsule, but dropping more quickly.

'They've brought their own pressure capsules,' Gisella realized.

The Doctor nodded. 'The question is, who's going to get down to the base first – us or them? We're in the lead, but they're going faster.'

He worked the sonic screwdriver again, and the speed and distances appeared next to their own

Activity

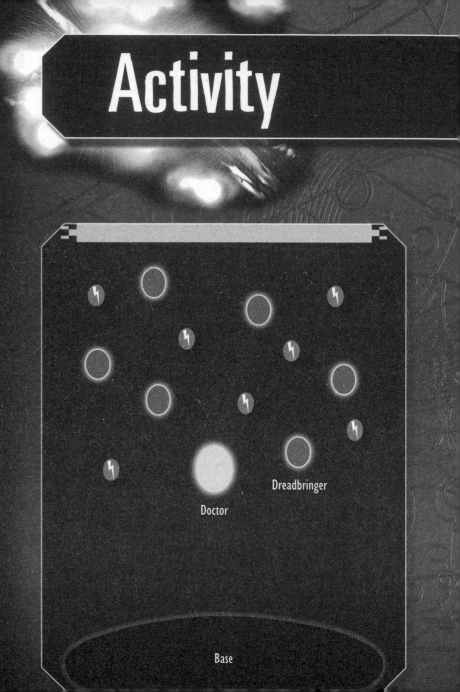

Dreadbringer

Doctor

Base

The Doctor's capsule:

Distance to Base: 450 metres
Speed: 150 metres per minute

The Dreadbringer's capsule:

Distance to Base: 700 metres
Speed: 175 metres per minute

Which capsule will reach the Base first?

_____

capsule and the Dreadbringer capsule that was closest to them.

'Well,' said Gisella, 'there's your answer. Who are these Dreadbringers?'

'They're the military and law enforcement arm of a people called the Darksmith Collective, from the planet Karagula.' The Doctor was watching Gisella carefully as he spoke. 'You've heard of the Darksmiths, I'm sure.'

'Have I?'

The Doctor sighed. 'Oh, stop playing games. We're neither of us children, despite appearances. So stop being so childish. You know full well who the Darkmsiths are, and I think you know why they've sent the Dreadbringers.'

Gisella turned away. 'Yes,' she said quietly. 'They've sent them to get me.'

'Exactly,' the Doctor nodded. Then he paused. 'To…what? No, no, no – why do you think that? Why would they want you? It's *me* they want. They're after the …' He stopped. 'Never mind,' he said. 'You really think they're after *you*?'

Gisella turned back, and the Doctor could see how scared she looked suddenly. 'Does it matter? Whichever of us they want, they'll tear the Base apart to find us. And we've got just one minute from when we arrive back in the Green Area before the first Dreadbringer capsule docks with the same airlocks.'

The Doctor brandished his sonic screwdriver. 'Unless we can stop them docking somehow.'

'You really think you can stop them?' Gisella asked.

'I think we have to try.'

Captain Strova. Privates Lenk and Rodoff and Hank were all waiting outside the capsule as the doors slid open.

'The Blaska are still heading for the living area,' Strova explained, her voice filtered through the mask, but still clear. 'And there's something following you down.'

'We know,' Gisella said.

'Well, whoever they are, they might try to force their way in.'

'They will,' the Doctor said grimly.

'Then you'd better get kitted up,' Strova told him, pointing to two more sets of breathing apparatus.

Gisella started to put hers on, but the Doctor ignored the masks and tanks and ran to the nearest control console. 'I'm sealing the airlocks shut,' he said. 'It won't keep them out, but it might slow them down.'

As he spoke there was the sound of a muffled explosion from somewhere outside.

'Or not,' Hank said.

'Back to your gloomy self, then?' the Doctor said. 'That's good to see. Right then...' He turned to face the others. 'There is a way out of here. The way I came in.' He held up his hand to stop them interrupting. 'Not a pressure capsule, well, not really. The problem is it's here...'

The Doctor pointed to the storage area where the TARDIS had landed.

'That's pretty close to where the Blaska are,' Lenk pointed out.

The Doctor nodded. 'And we can be sure the Dreadbringers will be close behind us, too.' He looked meaningfully at Gisella. 'Whatever they are actually after, we can assume they'll follow us. So let's not waste time debating it, and get going.'

'There's a service stairway here,' Rodoff said, showing the Doctor on the plan. 'We can get to it through the access corridor outside.'

'So what are we waiting for?' Captain Strova

demanded. She had opened an upright locker close to the door, and she took out a large gun shaped like a futuristic rifle.

'I'm not taking a gun,' the Doctor told her. 'I never carry weapons.'

'That's fine,' Strova said. 'Because I'm not offering you one.'

There was another explosion, this time from much closer. The wall close to the pressure capsule was glowing a deep red. As they all watched, a section of the metal peeled away and slid to the floor.

'The Dreadbringers are breaking through,' Gisella said.

With a tremendous crash, the exposed wall behind the missing section exploded. Smoke and flame erupted into the room, and the first of the Dreadbringers leaped through.

Out of the Frying Pan...

Before the smoke had cleared, the Doctor was making a final adjustment at one of the consoles. Then he was running with everyone else for the huge lead-lined doors.

Strova hit the opening code, and the doors began to swing open. An energy blast smashed into the wall close by, blowing out chunks of metal. As soon as there was room, Strova pushed Gisella through the gap between the opening doors. Lenk, Hank and Rodoff followed.

The Doctor waited for Strova, but she pushed him ahead of her, then turned and fired a long burst of energy from her gun. She didn't wait to see what effect it had, but dived after the Doctor.

On the other side of the doors, the Doctor was using his sonic screwdriver on the number pad.

It exploded in a shower of sparks, and the doors swung rapidly shut again.

'What are you doing?' Hank asked.

'Sorry, making work for you I expect. I told the systems that the reactor was about to explode. It's closed off the area. Should keep the Dreadbringers shut in for a bit.'

'And what do we do now?' Rodoff said. 'We've got monsters rampaging through the base, and alien soldiers behind us.'

The Doctor led the way at a brisk walk. 'Before we left,' he explained, 'I opened a few of the watertight doors between the Blaska and the living area.'

'You let them through?' Strova was appalled. 'Why?

'Because that way they didn't have to break through the doors. And once they were through I closed them again.'

'Good thinking,' Gisella said.

'Why?' Lenk asked. 'He's just let the monsters through.'

'But he stopped the base from flooding,' Gisella told him. 'The Doctor let the Blaska through, and the area filled with water from the ocean outside. But then he closed the watertight doors behind them. So the only water that can get to the living area is what was trapped between those doors.'

'Maybe the Blaska can only live in the water,' Hank said.

'Careful, you're getting optimistic again.' The Doctor thought of the enormous Blaska that had tried to drag the TARDIS below the ice when he first arrived. 'I think they'll be quite happy without being submerged. Sorry about that.'

They paused to open a watertight door. Once they were all through, the Doctor closed it again behind them. He worked the sonic screwdriver, locking the door so it couldn't be opened from the other side.

'So where are we going?' Strova demanded as they set off along the next section of corridor.

'Storage bay close to the living area. Where you first found me, Hank. There's something there we need if we're going to get out of here alive.'

From behind them came the sound of a tremendous explosion. The whole base shook under the force of the blast. The sound slowly died away.

'I think we should hurry,' the Doctor said. 'That'll be the Dreadbringers, and I doubt if they're very happy with us for locking them in the reactor area.'

Hank knew the base better than any of them, and led the way up through the levels and across towards the living area. Behind them, they could all hear the rumble of explosions as the Dreadbringers blasted their way through the doors the Doctor had locked to slow them down.

'Nearly there,' Hank announced. 'If we can get through the next section, we can cut through the Art Gallery.'

'You have an art gallery?' the Doctor asked.

'Sort of. You remember those pieces that Rodoff found in the cave?' Gisella said.

'Ornaments. Extruded volcanic sediment or whatever it was. You had it dotted about in the living area,' the Doctor recalled.

'I thought we might be able to sell it on Minima. Decorative objects, sculptures, whatever,' Rodoff explained. 'All profits put back into the research we're doing here, of course.'

'If we ever get out of here,' Lenk added.

'Anyway,' Strova said, 'there's a load of it stored in what we call the Art Gallery.'

'A trip that's educational and cultural as well as deadly dangerous,' the Doctor said. 'Just my sort of thing. Can't wait. Allons-y!'

They hurried to open the next door, aware that the sounds of explosions were getting steadily and rapidly closer.

'What do these Dreadbringers want?' Strova asked. 'Why are they here?'

The Doctor and Gisella exchanged glances. 'I'm afraid they're after me,' the Doctor said.

'Oh great,' Hank told him.

'So why are *we* running?' Lenk wondered.

'Because to get to me, they'll kill anyone and anything that gets in their way,' the Doctor said. 'You can't be a passive observer and just watch where the Dreadbringers are concerned. They'll rip this place apart to get me, and never mind who else dies as a result.'

'But once they've got you,' Rodoff said slowly, 'would they just leave?'

The Doctor stared at him. 'They might,' he said calmly. 'Or they might not. I for one don't want to find out. Do you?'

Rodoff looked away.

'Let's get this door open,' Gisella said. She helped Strova with the locking wheel.

The door opened suddenly and quickly. A tide of murky water rushed through.

'Shut it!' Hank yelled.

But the Doctor was shaking his head. 'No, no, no. It's OK. There's not much.'

He was right. The water sloshed across the floor, but it was soon only a few millimetres deep, like a shallow puddle.

'Looks like your plan with the doors worked, Doctor,' Gisella said.

'Looks like it did,' he agreed happily.

They hurried along the corridor, pausing only so the Doctor could close and seal the door behind them.

'The Art Gallery is just along here,' Hank said as they approached a junction with another corridor.

But before he had finished speaking, there was an echoing squeal of sound. Something huge and slimy slid round the end of the other corridor, blocking the way. A tentacle shot out, knocking Lenk off his feet. Strova yelled in surprise and loosed off a rapid series of energy bolts.

The tentacle whipped back. But not for long. Almost immediately, several more started to snake along the corridor.

'Back the way we came?' Hank suggested.

'Slight problem,' the Doctor said. 'I just locked and sealed the door, we're trapped.'

'Can't you unseal it?' Gisella said.

'If I had time.'

A Blaska was heaving itself down the corridor towards them now. Tentacles reached out, probing the air. Strova fired again, but after just one long energy burst, the gun stuttered to a halt.

'Out of charge,' she complained. In frustration she threw the gun at the nearest tentacle.

The tentacle curled round the weapon, squeezing and bending it, until the gun snapped in half with a sound like a stick breaking.

'The only way is back,' Rodoff pointed out. 'You'll have to work fast, Doctor.'

They turned and ran back down the corridor.

But before they reached the door, smoke started to curl round its edges.

'Down!' the Doctor yelled.

They all hurled themselves to the floor, just as the door at the end of the corridor exploded in flames. Dreadbringers leaped through, bringing up their long, thin weapons.

Behind the Doctor and his friends, tentacles

lashed out, slamming into the walls and floor.

'What now?' Gisella shouted above the noise.

'Now we die,' Hank told her. 'There's nowhere left to run.'

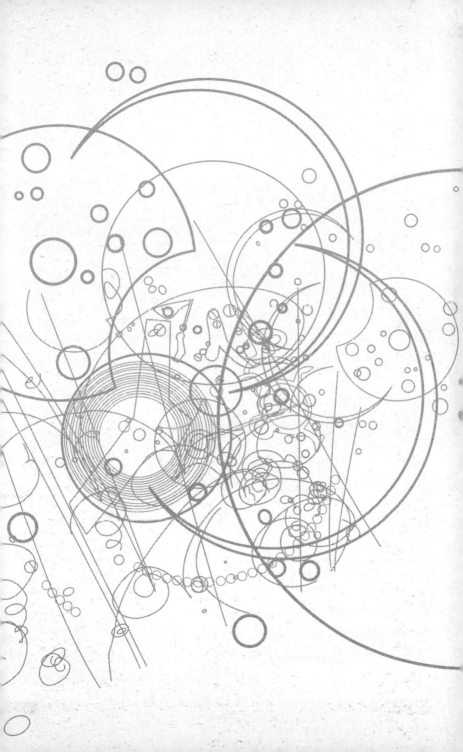

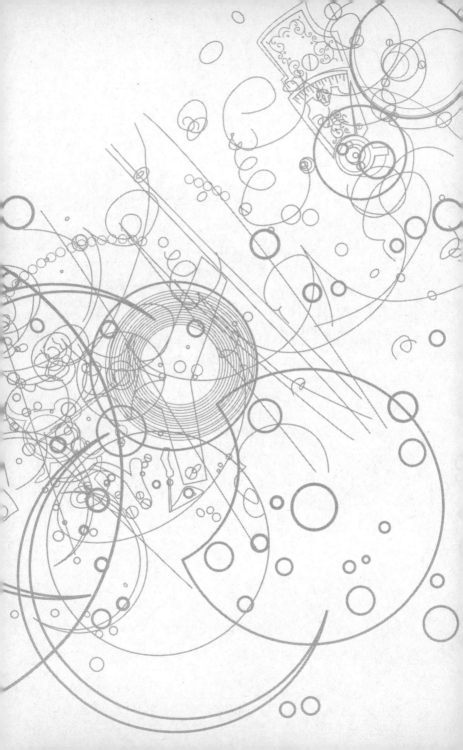

...Into the Fire

They were caught between the Dreadbringers at one end of the corridor, and the Blaska advancing from the other.

'There's always somewhere to run,' the Doctor said. 'I'm an expert at running – trust me, I know.'

'Trust you?' Rodoff said incredulously. 'It's because of you that we're in this mess.'

'Excuse me?' the Doctor shot back. 'It's because of me that you're still alive.' He pointed at the advancing Dreadbringers. 'They might be here because of me.' He turned and pointed at the tentacles writhing along the corridor from the other direction. 'But they're not. Without me you'd have drowned.'

'Doesn't matter how we die,' Hank said. 'Not really. Because it's going to happen.'

'Not on my watch,' the Doctor insisted. 'I just

need to find a piece of wall where the metal has been weakened.'

They had been lucky so far, hidden in the smoke from the exploding door. But the smoke was clearing. The Dreadbringers would see them any moment, if the powerful tentacles of the Blaska didn't grab and crush them first.

The first Dreadbringers were advancing cautiously along the corridor. They could hear the shrieks and squeals of the Blaska, and fired into the smoke. The wall close to the Doctor blackened and charred and dripped molten metal.

'That'll do it,' the Doctor announced. 'Everyone get down.' He had his sonic screwdriver out and aimed it at the blackened section of wall. Where the metal had melted and peeled away, rivets and fixing screws were visible – holding the section of corridor in place. 'Can you keep the Dreadbringers back for a bit?' the Doctor asked Strova.

She smiled down at him with grim satisfaction. 'No need. I think they've upset our Blaska friend.'

The energy blasts from the Dreadbringers' weapons scythed down the corridor. Apart from the shot that had hit the wall close to the Doctor, the Dreadbringers were aiming down the middle

– hoping their blasts would catch anyone trying to escape. What they actually hit was the approaching Blaska.

The creature roared and screeched in pain and anger. Tentacles lashed out, slamming down the corridor at the source of its pain. The first Dreadbringer ran straight into one of the larger tentacles, and was knocked off his feet. Moments later, another tentacle wrapped round his leg, dragging him rapidly down the corridor.

The Dreadbringer gave a scream of surprise and fear. He was firing his staff-like weapon at the tentacle. The Blaska's flesh blackened and scorched, but it held on. More tentacles wrapped round the Dreadbringer, slowly crushing the life from him. There was an ominous crack as his battle armour gave way.

The other Dreadbringers were hanging back now, uncertain what lay ahead. Through the clearing smoke they had caught a confused view of tentacles and the bulbous body of the Blaska. Now they regrouped, preparing to fire a concentrated volley of blasts at whatever was attacking them.

'This would be thrilling,' Gisella said, 'if we weren't caught in the middle of it.'

'Not for much longer,' the Doctor told her as he worked. One of the fixing screws fell from the wall, then another. Rivets popped out and scattered across the corridor.

'I think we can pull it away,' Strova said. She gestured for Lenk and Rodoff to help her. Together they heaved at the large metal plate. It pulled away from the wall slightly, but not enough.

'There's still something holding it in place,' Rodoff gasped as he strained with the effort.

'Magnetic clamps,' Hanks said. He pulled a small device from the pocket of his overalls. 'Here, let me.'

Hank ran the device along each side of the plate. As he did so, the magnetics holding the plate in place shut off and it peeled away from the wall. Behind it was darkness.

But the Doctor didn't hesitate. 'Right – all of you get inside.' He pushed Gisella through first.

The corridor was alive with energy bursts now. They seared into the Blaska's tentacles and body, and the smoke thickened and darkened.

The Doctor was the last through the hole they'd made in the wall. He dragged the metal plate back into place, and Hank reset the magnetics to hold the metal plate securely.

'With luck, they'll never realize what happened,' the Doctor said.

'Maybe they won't even realize we were ever there,' Lenk said.

'Not sure we'll get that lucky.' The Doctor worked his sonic screwdriver again, the light illuminating the room they were in. 'Where are we?' he wondered.

'Welcome to the Art Gallery,' Gisella said.

The Doctor looked round. They were in a large storage area, filled with free-standing shelves. Most of the shelves held boxes and crates, folders and files. But one whole section, close to where they were standing, had been turned into a display.

The shelves in this display section held pieces of the coral-like volcanic rock. There must have been a hundred pieces, varying in shape and size. They were also different colours – some dull, others startlingly bright.

'This must have taken you a while to collect,' the Doctor said. He put on his glasses and looked carefully along one of the shelves, examining the different pieces.

'We all brought back odd bits from survey

missions outside,' Lenk said.

'Then Rodoff found this cave that was full of the stuff,' Strova added.

'I was fixing new probes,' Rodoff explained. 'When I was done, I just filled the buggy with the stuff. Like I said, I think people will pay a lot for it.'

The Doctor was nodding thoughtfully. 'Then the Blaska started to get nasty, that right?'

'I guess so.'

'What are you thinking, Doctor?' Gisella asked.

The Doctor shrugged. 'I'm not sure.' He stood very still for a moment, listening. 'I'm thinking it's got very quiet outside, though.'

They all stood listening. 'Have they gone?' Hank wondered. 'The Blaska and those soldier things?'

The Doctor sniffed. 'Doubt it.' He took out the stethoscope he kept in his jacket pocket and went back to the section of wall where they had come in. He pressed the end of the stethoscope against the wall and listened through the earpieces.

'Anything?' Gisella asked.

'I think the Blaska has moved away,' the Doctor said. 'But there's something happening out there. Time we were going, I think.'

'The door's over here,' Hank called from the

other side of the Art Gallery display area. 'Your storage area is just through the next section.'

'If we ever make it,' Lenk muttered.

'Doctor!' Strova called urgently. 'The wall – it's getting hot!'

Behind her, a whole section of the wall was glowing red. As the Doctor watched, it started to blister and bubble. 'The Dreadbringers are burning their way in,' he realized.

'They've worked out where we went,' Rodoff said.

'Or they're just trying to find a way to get round the Blaska,' the Doctor pointed out.

'Let's get going, then,' Gisella told them.

The Doctor hurried after the others towards the door. But as he passed the display of volcanic rocks, he paused. A thought struck him, and he put the stethoscope back in his ears, pressed the end to one of the pieces of rock.

'Come on, Doctor!' Captain Strova shouted.

'No, no, hang on – this could be important.'

'It's just a rock,' Rodoff insisted. 'I carried it here myself. They're all just rocks,' he said as the Doctor moved on to press his stethoscope to another one.

'Really? Is that what you think?' The Doctor was folding up his stethoscope thoughtfully. 'If it's just

89

a rock, why's it got a heartbeat?'

'What?!' Gisella said. 'Are you sure?'

The Doctor was staring at the rock he'd just been listening to. 'I don't need to be sure. Look.' he pointed, and they could all see that the rock was moving. It was shuddering on the shelf. One of the nodules on the side cracked and fell away. Something was pushing its way through from inside.

The back wall of the room was bright orange, molten metal running down it and pooling on the floor as the Dreadbringers burned their way in.

There was a sudden thud from the main door close to where Strova and Hank were standing. The metal bulged inwards. The tip of a tentacle forced its way through, pushing the door open to reveal the hideous Blaska on the other side.

But everyone's attention was now on the lump of strangely-shaped rock. The outside was cracking and falling away like an eggshell. And a mass of tiny tentacles forced their way out.

The Hatching

'It's an egg,' Gisella realized. 'They're *all* eggs. Blaska eggs.'

'Which is why the Blaska want them so badly,' the Doctor said. 'They're just protecting their children. Now these eggs can sense that mummy and daddy are close by.'

The creature in the doorway was forcing its way into the room with its tentacles stretched out. They rippled and curled across the floor and through the air, searching out the lumps of rock that were really eggs, and gently stroking them.

'Checking the kids are all right,' the Doctor murmured.

'Which is more than we are,' Captain Strova said. 'Look!'

She pointed to the back wall of the room. The whole of one section had been burned away, and through the growing hole the dark shapes of the Dreadbringers were clearly visible.

'You know what we need?' the Doctor said.

'Surprise us,' Lenk told him.

'A huge big gun?' Rodoff suggested.

'Divine intervention,' Hank muttered, jumping to one side to avoid being swiped by a Blaska tentacle.

'We need a plan,' the Doctor told them. 'A really good plan. A genius plan that's so clever it's got its own TV chat show. And you know what?' he went on, 'I just happen to have that plan.'

The first Dreadbringer was pushing his way through the hole in the wall. He raised his staff. The end glowed red.

'It had better be a quick plan,' Strova said.

'Quick as this,' the Doctor told her. He grabbed the nearby Blaska egg that was already hatching. The thin tentacles twisted and curled as the small Blaska inside tried to push its way out. It was making a high-pitched squealing sound that was almost drowned out by the noise of the adult creature searching for it. But the adult seemed to hear or sense it, and a tentacle whipped across the room towards the Doctor.

Before the tentacle reached him, the Doctor

turned and threw the baby Blaska and its egg at the advancing Dreadbringer.

'Here, catch!'

Surprised, the Dreadbringer instinctively caught it. His staff deflected as he moved, the energy bolt burning into the ceiling. The Dreadbringer stared down at the wriggling creature in its gauntleted hand. Dark eyes glistened behind the visor of its helmet.

A moment later, a massive tentacle slammed into the Dreadbringer, knocking him back against the wall.

The Blaska was rolling forwards, squelching across the room to save its child. The Doctor was rolling more of the strange eggs across the floor towards the Dreadbringers now advancing into the room. Then he pressed himself back against the side wall, shouting for everyone else to do the same.

As soon as the Blaska was past them, they ran for the door. Behind them they could hear the shrieks of the Blaska, the cries of the Dreadbringers, the sound of energy bolts and the high-pitched wails of the hatching Blaska babies.

'Where to now?' Hank demanded as soon as they were out of the room.

'There will be more Blaska on their way,' the Doctor said. 'They must be able to sense their eggs.' He turned to Rodoff. 'You should never have taken them!'

Rodoff looked pale. 'I didn't know,' he said. 'How could I have known?'

'Humans!' the Doctor snapped. 'You just have to interfere, don't you. Can't leave well alone. Taking things that aren't yours.' He hesitated. 'Or am I thinking of someone else there. Never mind. Right, we have to get rid of the Dreadbringers before they harm the Blaska. Those creatures are just trying to rescue and protect their young. They don't deserve this.'

'Your storage area is just along there,' Hank said, pointing along the corridor.

'And the main living area is back this way,' Strova told them.

'Good. Next part of the plan,' the Doctor said. 'You lot get to the living area. Seal yourselves in. Make sure it's completely airtight, watertight and everything else tight.'

'Where are you going?' Gisella wanted to know.

'I'm going to open the outer airlock doors.'

'But that'll flood the whole base,' Lenk said.

'And flush out the Dreadbringers. The Blaska and their young can swim away and go home. The Dreadbringers will evacuate. And they won't come back.'

'Why not? Strova asked.

'Because what they're after won't be here any more, that's why.'

Hank was shaking his head. 'There's no way you can open those outer doors. They're deadlock sealed and you need remote authorisation.'

'What sort of authorisation?'

'Eye pattern, from one of the senior crew,' Strova said.

'And the only remote systems are in the Machine Room. You'll never get back there.'

'I could open the door myself, by hand,' the Doctor said.

'You could,' Gisella told him. 'But you'd drown.'

The Doctor nodded thoughtfully. 'Good point. Probably best to find another way if possible then. How are the main systems in the Machine Room connected to the airlock doors, Hank?'

'Encoded wireless network protocol, why?'

The Doctor grinned. 'Because I have some equipment of my own that can hack into that.'

'If you had an eye print,' Gisella pointed out.

'True.' The Doctor pointed at Strova. 'You, get everyone to the living area and seal it off.' He turned to Gisella. 'And as you're the most senior person here, I'm guessing your eye print will do the trick. So you'd better come with me.'

Gisella looked round the TARDIS control room in surprise. 'It's so big!'

'Clever isn't it?' the Doctor said. He hurried to the controls.

'What's that hammer for?' Gisella asked as she joined him.

'Oh sometimes I have to make very delicate adjustments, and sometimes I have to be rather more heavy handed,' the Doctor grinned. 'The hammer's for the delicate work.' He turned his attention to the screen over the controls. 'Here we are, I'm accessing the wireless systems.'

'You can just hack in?'

'Well, there are some security systems we have to get through.' He turned the screen so she could see too. 'Any idea what the solutions to these protocol questions are?'

'The security system was devised by Varlos,'

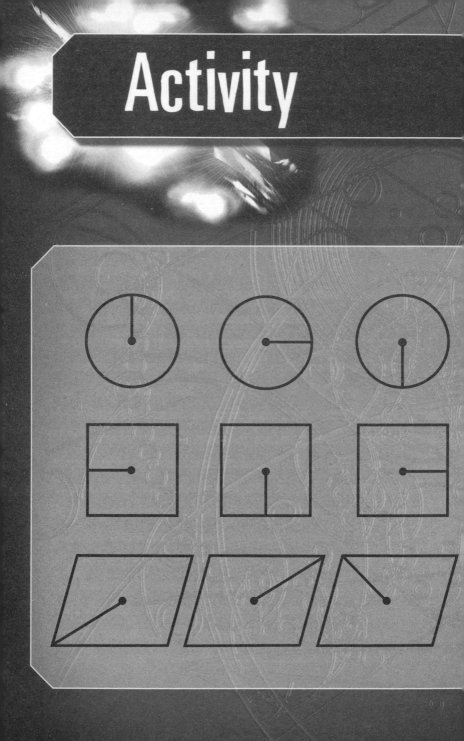

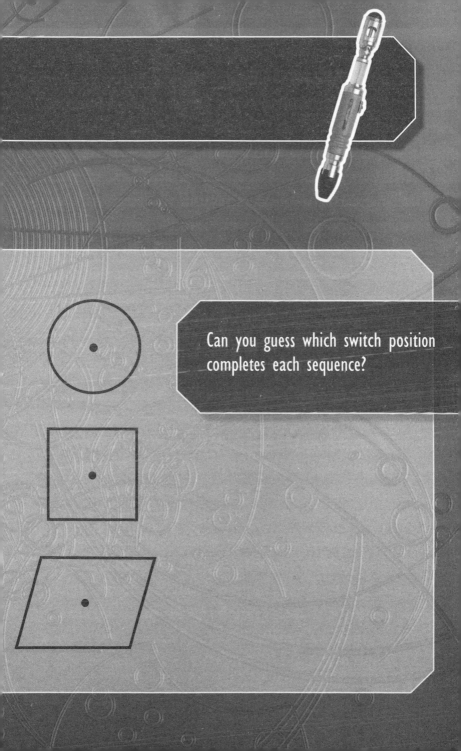

Can you guess which switch position completes each sequence?

Gisella said. 'It's a logical sequence. In each case you have to set the switch to the next position in the sequence.'

'I can see that,' the Doctor said. His hands blurred as he worked rapidly at the TARDIS controls. 'That look right to you?' he asked as he completed the last sequence.

'It does.'

The Doctor pressed a button. The screen cleared, and a new image appeared. It was a picture of an eye, with the instruction:

Provide Valid Eye Print To Proceed

'Looks like it's your turn,' the Doctor told Gisella. He showed her a small camera close to the screen. 'Just look into this. It'll take a little while to upload the image of your eye.'

While they waited, Gisella staring unblinking into the camera, the Doctor adjusted various TARDIS controls.

'So Varlos set up the systems. You seem to know a lot about him. Maybe there's a logical reason why you'd know so much, just as it was logical to set the first switch to point to the left, the second to point straight up, and the third to point to the bottom right corner.'

'What do you mean?' Gisella asked.

'I just mean, that I think you know a lot more about Varlos than you are telling me.'

The TARDIS gave a ping, and the screen changed again. This time, it said:

Access Granted

'It will only take a minute to give it the instructions to open the airlocks,' the Doctor said. 'Let's hope Captain Strova and the others are ready and safe in the living area.'

As he finished speaking, the TARDIS shuddered. The Doctor worked a control, and part of the screen changed to show the storage area outside the TARDIS. A group of Dreadbringers were firing their weapons straight at the screen – straight at the TARDIS.

'We may not have a minute,' Gisella said. 'The Dreadbringers are trying to get in!'

Taken at the Flood

The Doctor calmly watched the Dreadbringers firing at the TARDIS.

'Don't worry,' he said. 'They'll never get through that door. That door will keep out an army of Pyroviles, never mind a few Dreadbringers.'

'Maybe so, but we're trapped in here now,' Gisella said.

'We'll be trapped by the water soon.' The Doctor had already completed the final sequence to open the outer airlocks. The TARDIS screen was showing a countdown over the images of the Dreadbringers outside:

10

'Let me open a communication link to the living area,' the Doctor said.

9

'If Strova and the others aren't there yet, we can

105

hold the countdown till they're safe.'

8

The TARDIS beeped as he opened the link.

7

'Captain Strova? Are you there? Can you hear me?' the Doctor asked.

6

There was silence from the other end.

5

'Maybe we should wait,' Gisella said. The TARDIS lurched again.

4

Then a crackly voice said: 'This is Captain Strova. We can hear you loud and clear.'

3

'Thank goodness,' Gisella said. 'Are you ready? We're about to open the airlocks.'

2

'You'd better hurry up. There's a group of Dreadbringers outside, trying to get in.'

1

'Just give me a second,' the Doctor said.

0 – *Outer Airlocks Opening*

'There you go.'

Even inside the TARDIS, they could hear the distant rumble of the water flooding into the base. The Doctor could imagine it forcing its way through the airlocks – icy cold water crashing into the base, rushing along the corridors and through the rooms and storage areas.

A schematic plan of the base appeared on the screen. It showed the progress of the water flooding through. It showed the Blaska as small unidentified life-blips. A mass of tiny dots surrounded the three creatures – the eggs and hatching children.

'The Blaska are leaving,' Gisella said, pointing. The life-blips were moving back towards the incoming water, making for the open airlocks.

'They've got what they came for,' the Doctor said. 'Which is more than the Dreadbringers can say.'

He flipped the screen back to the view of the storage area outside. A sudden cascade of water was crashing through the doors. The TARDIS rocked under the impact. The Dreadbringers were swept aside. There was a confused image of their bodies being swept away in the tide of foaming water.

'Will they drown?'

The Doctor shook his head. 'Their battle armour has built in life-support. Works in space, so it'll work under water. They have some way of detecting this, even when it's held in stasis.'

He pointed to a small metal box at the side of the console.

'What is it?'

'A Crystal.'

Gisella's eyes widened. 'The Eternity Crystal!'

The Doctor watched her carefully. 'You know about it?'

'A little. Just what Varlos told me.'

'You actually met Varlos?'

'A long time ago. Like I told you, I'm older than I look.'

'You must be,' the Doctor said. 'I need to find Varlos, I need him to tell me how I can destroy this Crystal rather than let the Darksmiths get it back. Will you help me?'

Gisella frowned. 'You'd let me come with you? To find Varlos?'

The Doctor nodded. 'If you tell me how you know him. If you tell me the truth – about Varlos and about the Eternity Crystal. Deal?'

'Hey Doctor!' Strova's voice came over the

TARDIS speakers. 'You OK?'

The Doctor didn't look away from Gisella. 'I'm fine,' he said. 'We're both fine. How are you lot doing?'

'All OK,' Strova reported. 'Rodoff says he's sorry about the Blaska, and Lenk says he's right to be sorry.'

'Good. And how's Hank?'

'He's complaining about the mess and all the repairs he'll have to do.'

'Sounds like he's all right, too. The Blaska have gone, and so have the Dreadbringers. I'll close the airlocks and pump the water out. Then Hank can get started. Oh, and Gisella has something to tell you.'

While the Doctor sorted out the airlocks and the pumps, Gisella told Strova she was leaving with the Doctor. She said a tearful goodbye, and promised she'd come back and see how they were doing soon. 'You're in charge till I get back.'

'Yes, Ma'am,' Strova said. 'And Doctor – thank you.'

'So where are we going, Gisella?' The Doctor was circling the TARDIS console, a manic bundle of energy and pinstripes jabbing out at the occasional switch and lever. 'Where can we find Varlos, then?'

Gisella was looking round, still in awe and amazement at the impossibly huge room. 'He went to Earth,' she said at last. 'I can give you the exact location.'

'And how would you know that?'

'He was going into retirement. He'd had enough of the Darksmiths and their plotting, scheming ways. He was scared of the Eternity Crystal, terrified of what he had created, and he knew he had to hide it away until he could work out how to destroy it. We managed to escape, and Varlos brought me here.'

The Doctor was surprised. 'You escaped too? From the Darksmiths? All those years ago?'

Gisella nodded. 'Varlos brought me here, to hide me like the Crystal. He wanted me far away, but he wanted the Crystal close enough that he could recover it when he knew how to destroy it.'

'But why would he hide *you*?' The Doctor was confused. 'Who are you, Gisella? Who are you really?'

Gisella sighed. 'I'm sorry Doctor, I really am.

But Varlos must have been dead for years. He left me here so long ago, and he was very old even then. I miss him so much. You see – I'm his daughter.'

To Be Continued...

TARDIS
Data Bank

The Darksmith Collective

Data accessed about the Darksmith Collective:

The Darksmiths of Karagula are the ultimate artisans. They can fashion the most extraordinary artefacts from the most ordinary materials. They can bend the physical world to their will, and manipulate the raw substance of reality itself.

Centuries ago, the Darksmith Collective received its most challenging and dangerous commission — to create life itself.

Project Details — *Classified, unable to access data*

Client — *Classified, unable to access data*

Brother Varlos

Brother Varlos was the greatest of the Darksmiths. It was said that he could reshape time and space and manipulate the atoms themselves so they would form new — even unheard-of — molecules.

So it was to Varlos that the Darksmith Collective gave this most difficult commission. But the final use of his invention was not divulged beyond the Darksmith Collective and their very special client who had commissioned this most secret project.

But when Varlos was finished, when he had finally worked out how to use the Eternity Crystal he had created, Varlos learned the identity of his clients.

Brother Varlos was so horrified that he retired from Karagula, going into hiding from the Darksmith Collective and their clients, and taking his awful discovery with him. He also took something else — another great secret...

To find out what events lie in store
for the Doctor and the mystery of the
Darksmith Legacy, look out for
The Vampire of Paris.
But for now, here is a taste of
things to come...

Terror at Midnight

'So where are we going, Gisella?' The Doctor was circling the TARDIS console, a manic bundle of energy and pinstripes jabbing out at the occasional switch and lever. 'Where can we find Varlos, then?'

Gisella was looking round, still in awe and amazement at the impossibly huge room. 'He went to Earth,' she said at last. 'I can give you the exact location.'

'And how would you know that?'

'He was going into retirement. He'd had enough of the Darksmiths and their plotting, scheming ways. He was scared of the Eternity Crystal, terrified of what he had created, and he knew he had to hide it away until he could work out how to destroy it. We managed to escape, and Varlos brought me here.'

The Doctor was surprised. 'You escaped too? From the Darksmiths? All those years ago?'

Gisella nodded. 'Varlos brought me here, to hide me like the Crystal. He wanted me far away, but he wanted the Crystal close enough that he could recover it when he knew how to destroy it.'

'But why would he hide *you*?' The Doctor was confused. 'Who are you, Gisella? Who are you really?'

Gisella sighed. 'I'm sorry Doctor, I really am. But Varlos must have been dead for years. He left me here so long ago, and he was very old even then. I miss him so much. You see – I'm his daughter.'

'Oh,' the Doctor stared. 'Oh Gisella, I'm sorry, I had no idea,' he reflected. 'Mainly because you didn't tell me. I get the feeling there's a lot you're not telling me, Gisella. But look, if you give me the exact location for Varlos, I can sort you out a happy family reunion in no time.'

'Paris,' said Gisella simply. 'The part called Montmartre, in the Earth-relative year 1895.'

The Doctor calculated. '1895, that's going back a bit. You were left for a long time, weren't you?' He slammed home the last lever and the TARDIS engines grated noisily into life. The Doctor grinned as Gisella looked around in alarm. 'What? That was a good take-off! Hold on tight!'

As he spoke, the TARDIS lurched – as if something very large had heard his command and thrown its arms around the vessel.

'Is that normal for this craft?' Gisella asked.

'Normal's not a word that goes well with me,' the Doctor admitted, checking some readouts. 'Looks like something's speeding through space and time behind us, riding the TARDIS' coat-tails.' He frowned. 'Or rather, box-tails. Outer plasmic shell-tails. Whatever! They're letting us tow them through the time Vortex.'

Gisella frowned. 'They're following us?'

'Trying to. But that's a dodgy business – because unless you know what you're doing, the time winds can spit you back out into reality at a trillion light-years per second...' He winced. 'As whoever was after us has just found out.'

'Who were they?' asked Gisella.

'Dunno,' said the Doctor grimly.

'Dreadbringers?'

The Doctor shook his head. 'They'd be ripped apart in the Vortex.'

'Then who?'

THE DARKSMITH LEGACY - *THE VAMPIRE OF PARIS*

'Well, if you see any large dents in nineteenth century Paris, try asking them.' The TARDIS came suddenly to rest. 'Aha! We're here!'

Nicholas rolled over on his hard mattress, listening to the other children snore and snuffle in their sleep. Twenty of them were crammed into one dark room, many squashed together on the hard tiled floor. Madame Misra's orphanage was damp, strict and smelly but it was better than being out on Paris' cobblestones.

A distant clock chimed midnight through the boarded up window.

'Better times are coming,' Nicholas told himself quietly. *In only five years a brand new century will begin*, he thought. *1900! I will be fourteen, a proper man. I'll go wherever I choose...*

There was a strange dragging, slithering noise from just outside the room.

SSSCRAPE...

I'll do whatever I want and no one will be able to stop me.

SSSSSSCRAPE...

The door handle squeaked in the dark as it turned slowly. Nicholas kept his eyes closed. Madame

Misra might cane you if she thought you were awake after candles-out. But what was she carrying? *SSSCRAPE...* He heard the sound again, like a heavy, sticky sack being dragged across the floor.

Then the screaming started.

Nicholas jumped up. The dark dormitory was bathed now in a faint, blood-red glow. Bodies and shadows seemed to mingle in a wild dance of terror as *something* moved through the mass of young boys, lashing out misshapen limbs, snapping inhuman jaws. Nicholas' ears rang with the shrieks of his friends. In a panic he tried to run for the door...

The screams around him were choking off into weird, feeble groans. Nicholas stumbled and fell. He looked up and saw two crimson eyes blazing in a hideous face. As a deformed claw reached out for his neck, Nicholas shrieked loudest of all...

DOCTOR · WHO

THE DARKSMITH LEGACY

'Collected' Party

POLICE PUBLIC CALL BOX

Celebrate the epic Darksmith Legacy experience with an out-of-this-world party to be held in a secret London location during the October half-term 2009, after the final exciting instalment has been published.

For your chance to win an exclusive ticket to this Doctor Who Extravaganza you must sign up at www.thedarksmithlegacy.com, complete the quest online and submit your details. We will let you know if you have been successful via email.

This will be a once in a lifetime opportunity to win lots of Doctor Who prizes and see scary monsters up-close...

...Don't miss out!

More party details will be revealed in another dimension on the Darksmith website so keep checking back for further updates. Full Terms and Conditions can also be found at www.thedarksmithlegacy.com.

DOCTOR · WHO

Fantastic free Doctor Who slipcase offer when you buy two Darksmith Legacy books!

Limited to the first 500 respondents!

To be eligible to receive your free slipcase, fill in your details on the form below and send along with original receipt(s) showing the purchase of two Darksmith Legacy books. The first 500 correctly completed forms will receive a slipcase.

Offer subject to availability. Terms and conditions apply. See overleaf for details.

DOCTOR · WHO

THE DARKSMITH LEGACY

www.thedarksmithlegacy.com

1 2 3 4 5 6 7 8 9 10

Cut Here — — — — — — — — — — — — — — — — — — —

Entry Form

Name: ....

Address: ....

Email: ....

Have you remembered to include your two original sales receipts? ⬡

I have read and agree to the terms and conditions overleaf. ⬡

Tick here if you don't want to receive marketing communications from Penguin Brands and Licensing. ⬡

Important – Are you over 13 years old?

If you are 13 or over just tick this box, you don't need to do anything else. ⬡

If you are under 13, you must get your parent or guardian to enter the promotion on your behalf. If they agree, please show them the notice below.

Notice to parent/guardian of entrants under 13 years old

If you are a parent/guardian of the entrant and you consent to the retention and use of the entrant's personal details by Penguin Brands and Licensing for the purposes of this promotion, please tick this box. ⬡

Name of parent/guardian: ....

Terms and Conditions

1. This promotion is subject to availability and is limited to the first 500 correctly completed respondents received.
2. This promotion is open to all residents aged 7 years or over in the UK, with the exception of employees of the Promoter, their immediate families and anyone else connected with this promotion. Entries from entrants under the age of 13 years must be made by a parent/guardian on their behalf.
3. The Promoter accepts no responsibility for any entries that are incomplete, illegal or fail to reach the promoter for any reason. Proof of sending is not proof of receipt. Entries via agents or third parties are invalid.
4. Only one entry per person. No entrant may receive more than one slipcase.
5. To enter, fill in your details on the entry form and send along with original sales receipt(s) showing purchase of two Doctor Who: The Darksmith Legacy books to: Doctor Who Slipcase Offer, Brands and Licensing, 80 Strand, London, WC2R 0RL.
6. The first 500 correctly completed entries will receive a slipcase.
7. Offer only available on purchases of Doctor Who: The Darksmith Legacy books.
8. Please allow 31 days for receipt of your slip case.
9. Slip cases are subject to availability. In the event of exceptional circumstances, the Promoter reserves the right to amend or foreclose the promotion without notice. No correspondence will be entered into.
10. All instructions given on the entry form, form part of the terms and conditions.
11. The Promoter will use any data submitted by entrants for only the purposes of running the promotion, unless otherwise stated in the entry details. By entering this promotion, all entrants consent to the use of their personal data by the Promoter for the purposes of the administration of this promotion and any other purposes to which the entrant has consented.
12. By entering this promotion, each entrant agrees to be bound by these terms and conditions.
13. The Promoter is Penguin Books Limited, 80 Strand, London WC2R 0RL.

Cut Here

Doctor Who Slipcase Offer
Brands and Licensing
80 Strand
London
WC2R 0RL